GUESS HOW MUCH I LOVE YOU

Written by

Sam McBratney

Illustrated by

Anita Jeram

WALKER BOOKS

AND SUBSIDIARIES

LONDON • BOSTON • SYDNEY • AUCKLAND

Little Nutbrown Hare, who was going to bed, held on tight to Big Nutbrown Hare's very long ears.

He wanted to be sure that Big
Nutbrown Hare was listening.
"Guess how much
I love you," he said.

"Oh, I don't think I could guess that,"
said Big Nutbrown Hare.

"This much," said Little
Nutbrown Hare, stretching out
his arms as wide as they could go.

Big Nutbrown Hare had even
longer arms. "But I love YOU
this much," he said.

Hmm, that is a lot, thought
Little Nutbrown Hare.

"I love you
as high as
I can reach,"
said Little
Nutbrown
Hare.

"I love you as high as *I* can reach," said Big Nutbrown Hare.

That is quite high, thought Little Nutbrown Hare. I wish I had arms like that.

Then Little
Nutbrown Hare
had a good idea.
He tumbled
upside down
and reached
up the tree
trunk with
his feet.

"I love you
all the way up
to my toes!"
he said.

"And *I* love you
all the way up
to your toes," said
Big Nutbrown Hare,
swinging him up
over his head.

"I love you
as high as
I can HOP!"
laughed Little
Nutbrown Hare,

bouncing up
and down.

"But I love you as high as
I can hop," smiled Big
Nutbrown Hare – and he
hopped so high that his ears
touched the branches above.

That's good
hopping,
thought
Little
Nutbrown
Hare.
I wish I
could hop
like that.

"I love you all the way down the
lane as far as the river," cried
Little Nutbrown Hare.

"I love you across the river
and over the hills," said
Big Nutbrown Hare.

That's very far, thought
Little Nutbrown Hare.

He was almost too sleepy
to think any more.

Then he looked beyond the
thorn bushes, out into the big

dark night. Nothing could
be further than the sky.

"I love you right up to
the MOON," he said,
and closed his eyes.

"Oh, that's far," said
Big Nutbrown Hare.
"That is very,
very far."

Big Nutbrown Hare settled
Little Nutbrown Hare
into his bed of leaves.

He leaned over
and kissed him
good night.

Then he lay down close by
and whispered with a smile,
"I love you right up to the moon –

AND BACK."